This Angelina Ballerina Annual belongs to

JULIAgwyn

Annual 2005

Contents

Written and edited by Brenda Apsley
Designed by Sally Metcalfe

Stories adapted from original scripts by Paul Larson,
Sally-Anne Lever, James Mason, Diane Redmond and Barbara Slade

Based on the text by Katharine Holabird
Illustrations by Helen Craig

Published in Great Britain in 2004 by Egmont Books Limited, 239 Kensington High Street, London W8 6SA.
Printed in Italy.
3 5 7 9 10 8 6 4
ISBN 1 4052 1387 6

Hello!

i've had a great year, with lots and lots of fun – and dancing, of course! i hope you enjoy reading all about my adventures in my new annual.

Angelina's home and

Angelina is a little white mouseling who lives in a village called Chipping Cheddar, in Mouseland. There are houses, shops, a school, and Angelina's favourite place – Miss Lilly's ballet school.

Angelina's home is an old cottage with a thatched roof and lots of old beams. It has a garden full of flowers, and climbing plants growing up the walls.

Through the bright red front door there's a sitting room with comfy chairs, and there's usually a cosy fire burning in the big fireplace.

Inside the green back door there's a big kitchen that's always full of nice smells.

Upstairs are the bedrooms. Angelina's is the one with a doll sitting on the window sill.

Angelina's family

Angelina's dad, **Mr Maurice Mouseling**, runs the local paper, the Mouseland Gazette. He's always making jokes, and loves playing his fiddle.

Angelina's mum is **Mrs Matilda Mouseling**. She's kind and loving, and when Angelina is upset or angry, she always knows just what to say to make things better. She makes Angelina's ballet costumes – and the best Cheddar cheese pies in Mouseland!

Angelina has a baby sister called **Polly**. She's cute and lovable, and Angelina thinks being a big sister is a whole lot of fun.

Angelina ... by Alice

Angelina Mouseling is my very best friend in all the world!

Angelina is a great dancer – much better than me! She has a big plan for a small mouseling, and that's to be a great ballerina one day. She's got natural talent, but she works hard, too, because she knows that making her dream come true won't be easy. But somehow I just know she'll do it.

Angelina loves fun and adventure, and so do I, so we have great times together. She's always getting us into some scrape or other. Some of them are funny, but some of them are scary, too!

Angelina tries hard to be good, but sometimes she likes to get her own way. She can be VERY stubborn at times – and I should know! But she's kind and thoughtful, too, and likes to help out if she can.

Angelina is ... Angelina!

Alice ... by Angelina

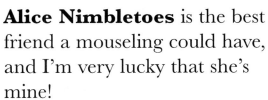

Alice Nimbletoes is the best friend a mouseling could have, and I'm very lucky that she's mine!

Alice is happy and jolly, and she always has a smile for me, no matter what I've done or how silly I've been! She has a heart of gold, and she laughs at the silliest things. Her giggles make everyone else want to laugh, too.

Alice likes to dance, but she's a bit clumsy sometimes. She says she doesn't know her left paw from her right! I may be a better dancer than Alice, but she's much cleverer than I am. She's always got her nose in some book or other, and she knows the most amazing things!

Alice is ... the best!

Angelina's photo album

Do you have a photo album? I love mine because I have pictures of all my family and my friends in it – and a few of my enemies, too! Here are some of my favourite pages.

This photo of Mum was taken in the summer. She made a big jug of orange juice for me and my friends.

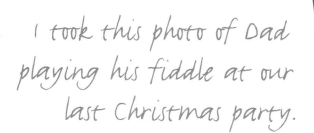

I took this photo of Dad playing his fiddle at our last Christmas party.

These pictures of my sister Polly show just how tiny she was – and how much she's grown!

Grandpa is old, and has to walk with a stick sometimes, but he's still full of fun, and he's a great storyteller.

Grandma is so sweet! she likes me to behave like a lady – just like her!

Mrs Hodgepodge lives next door. She loves her garden, but she doesn't like dancing, and she doesn't like noisy mouselings, so we're not always the best of friends!

This is my all-time hero — Miss Lilly. She's from Dacovia, and she wears wonderful dresses and scarves. Like me, she just loves to dance.

Isn't my cousin Henry a sweet little mouseling? He can be a pest sometimes, but I love him really.

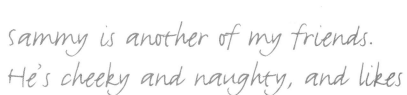

sammy is another of my friends. He's cheeky and naughty, and likes playing tricks on me, but I always find a way to pay him back.

William is one of my best friends. He's a bit shy – not like me! – and he sometimes gets his words mixed up when i'm around. Alice says it's because he has a crush on me!

Penelope and Priscilla are the Pinkpaws twins. They like to get their own way, and they have the best of everything – except the best dance steps.
They're mine!

The ballerina rag doll

1 One day, Angelina had some news for Alice. "Guess what," she said. "I'm going to help with Miss Lilly's new beginners' ballet class! Oh, I feel so grown up!"

2 When Angelina and Alice went to Mrs Thimble's shop to buy sweets, there was a box on the counter. "Don't forget my second-hand box, will you?" she said.

3 "Bring me any toys you've grown out of, and I'll sell them and buy food for hungry mouselings." Angelina nodded. "We'll spring-clean our toys!"

4 When she got home, Angelina sorted her toys into 'keep' and 'go' boxes. Her ballerina rag doll, Polka, went into the 'go' box. "She's babyish," said Angelina.

5 Later, Grandpa, Grandma and Angelina were looking through a photo album. "Look, it's you with Polka," said Grandpa. "I won her for you at the fair."

6 Grandpa smiled. "You promised me you'd never, ever lose her, didn't you?" Angelina put her paw to her mouth. "I did?" she said. "Yes, er ... of course I did."

7 Angelina rushed to Alice's house. "I've made a terrible mistake," she told her friend. "Come on, help me. We've got to get Polka back!"

8 But Polka had been sold! "Do you know who bought her?" asked Angelina. Mrs Thimble shook her head. "I'm sorry, dear," she said, "I can't remember."

9 Angelina was determined to find Polka. She put up 'LOST' posters with Polka's picture on them all over the village. But no one came to say they had her.

10 Angelina decided to go to every house and ask if anyone had seen Polka. All the villagers said no – except an elderly mouseling called Miss Twitchett.

11 "I did buy a lot of toys from Mrs Thimble," said Miss Twitchett. "I packed them all up, and sent them to the poor little orphan mouselings in Dacovia."

12 "Now what am I going to do?" Angelina said to Alice on the way home. "Dacovia is thousands of miles away!" Alice shrugged. "There's nothing you **can** do."

13 Next day, Angelina helped Miss Lilly with the beginners. The last to arrive was a tiny mouseling called Mary Greyfur. "Come, darlink!" said Miss Lilly.

14 Mary looked very shy, and held onto something very tightly in one paw. Angelina ran over to Mary and took her other paw. "Come with me," she said.

15 Angelina sat Mary with the others, and went back to stand with Miss Lilly. It was then that she saw what Mary was holding in her paw. It was Polka!

16 "Now skip, and skip!" said Miss Lilly as Angelina showed the little mouselings what to do. But Mary didn't join in. She just sat on the floor in the corner ...

17 While Miss Lilly talked to the class, Angelina went to talk to Mary. "I like your doll," she said. "Does she have a name?" Mary shook her head.

18 "Did someone give her to you?" asked Angelina. Mary nodded. "Miss Twitchett. I helped her wrap the toys, and she let me choose one."

19 "Well, actually, she's ..." said Angelina, then she stopped as Mary held up Polka to show her. "She's ... lovely, and she likes dancing. Can I show you?"

20 As Angelina started to dance, Mary handed Polka to her, and Angelina and Polka danced together, round and round, as Mary watched.

21 Then Mary stood up, took Polka from Angelina, and started to dance! Miss Lilly smiled. "Well done, my darlink!" she whispered to Angelina.

22 At the end of the class, Mary spoke to Angelina. "I want to dance like you," she said. "And I've got a name for my doll now. I'm going to call her Angelina!"

23 Later, Angelina told Grandpa about Polka. "I'm proud of you," said Grandpa. "That was a very grown-up thing to do. Polka's with someone who needs her."

24 Angelina hugged Grandpa. "Now," he said, bowing, "will you dance with **me**?" Angelina nodded. Can you guess what they danced? Yes – the polka!

Angelina's year: spring

Sorting out my old toys and books for Mrs Thimble's second-hand box wasn't the only spring-cleaning I did this year. One day at ballet school Miss Lilly said how untidy everything was. "Look!" she said. "The floor is very dusty and there are books of music and ballet shoeboxes everywhere. What a mess! We must do some spring-cleaning after class. Would any of you like to help, darlinks?"

I put my paw up right away, and so did my friend, Alice. "We'll help!" we both said.

The Pinkpaws twins kept their paws by their sides. "Cleaning?" said Priscilla. "I don't think so!"

"You won't find **me** scrubbing floors!" Penelope whispered.

I don't usually like cleaning – it's boring – but we had a really good time. Somehow Miss Lilly manages to make even the most dull jobs fun. She got a bucket of water and a scrubbing brush to clean the floor. "Now, you must wear these to protect your precious paws," she said, and she gave me a pair of red rubber gloves to wear. They were SO smart! Then instead of telling me what to do, she sang it, just as she does when she's teaching us new steps.

"Forward and back," sang Miss Lilly, "and one and two!"

I didn't know scrubbing the floor could be so much fun! And guess what? Yes – I got to keep the red gloves!

Miss Lilly was very pleased that Alice and I had helped with the spring-cleaning. "You deserve a special treat as a thank you," she said. "Would you like me to teach you a special ribbon dance, darlinks?"

Would we? You bet! We had a special private lesson, and Miss Lilly gave us these amazing dresses with matching ribbons. At the next class we performed the dance for the others. Were those Pinkpaws twins jealous? You should have seen their faces!

I love flowers! When I saw all the new spring pansies in Mrs Hodgepodge's garden, I bent down to have a closer look at their little faces – and fell over!

Mrs Hodgepodge was NOT pleased – until I said I'd show her how sorry I was by helping her plant her new plants. That brought a smile to her face!

I love flowers!

Spring fun

I love spring. It's the time of year when everything is green and new!

Look carefully at the spring picture. Count the number of each item, and write your answers in the flower shapes.

Miss Lilly comes to dinner

It was a warm summer's day, and Angelina's mum and dad were busy in the kitchen, making an extra-large cheese pie. Angelina was busy, too. She filled a vase with water and put some pretty wild flowers in it. Miss Lilly was coming to dinner, and she wanted everything to be just right.

Angelina danced round and round the kitchen. "Miss Lilly's coming to dinner," she sang. "Miss Lilly's coming to dinner!"

Later on, at ballet school, Angelina told Alice about the

cheese pie. She didn't notice that the Pinkpaws twins were listening – and laughing.

Just then, Miss Lilly arrived. "Sorry I'm a little late, my darlinks," she said. "I was at the theatre last night at a charity gala for my homeland, Dacovia."

Priscilla Pinkpaws winked at her sister. "Our mum was there, too," she said.

"Yes, they both went to the Mouseski Restaurant after the show," said Penelope. "It's so elegant."

"And Miss Lilly said her dish of Corn Royale was just D-I-V-I-N-E!" added Priscilla.

After ballet class, Angelina walked home with Alice, her best friend. She looked worried.

"The Mouseski Restaurant is so ... GRAND!" said Angelina.

"So?" said Alice. "It might be grand, but you'd never get one of your mum's yummy cheese pies there!"

"**Exactly**!" said Angelina. "And look at our cottage. It's so ... small!"

Later that afternoon, Angelina made her mum try on a fancy blue dress. It was very tight. "Do I have to wear this?" asked Mrs Mouseling.

"Yes, Mum," said Angelina. "Miss Lilly's used to having dinner with ... kings ... and queens! And Mum, can you make Corn Royale for her? It's her favourite."

"But I haven't got a recipe," said Mrs Mouseling. "Or the things I'll need."

"I'll get them!" said Angelina. "Please, Mum?"

"Oh, all right, Angelina," said Mrs Mouseling.

A little while later, Angelina and Alice were in the library, looking at cookery books.

"YES!" said Angelina, taking a book from the shelf. "This is what we need, *The Mouseski Restaurant Cook Book*. We need some music for Dad to play, too. Here we are – *Dacovian Polkas*."

Next, Angelina and Alice went to Mrs Thimble's shop.

"Can we have four corn cobs, please?" said Angelina. "And some green Dacovian tomatoes?"

"I've got the corn," said Mrs Thimble. "But I don't have **green** tomatoes. I've got some nice ripe red ones. Will they do?"

"Yes," said Angelina, looking at her list. "Now, do you have Dacovian Royal Blue cheese?"

"Oh no, I don't sell fancy stuff like that!" said Mrs Thimble. "But I've got Mouseland Cheddar."

"That's fine," said Angelina. "Come on, Alice."

A few minutes later, Angelina and Alice were riding home on their bikes. Their baskets were full of books and shopping, and Angelina's had the big bag of tomatoes wobbling on top ...

"Come on, Alice!" said Angelina, pedalling as fast as she could. She sped around a corner – and almost ran into the Pinkpaws twins! She swerved, and the books and shopping in her basket flew out.

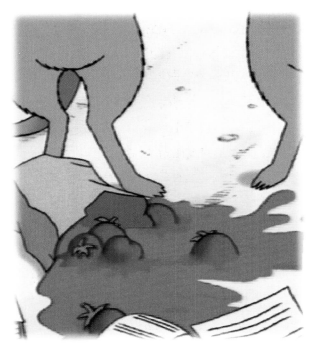

SPLAT!
SPLOSH!
"Oh nooooo!" said Angelina.

The ripe red tomatoes hit Penelope and Priscilla, and splattered all over them and the road.

"Ugh!" said Priscilla.

"Yuk!" said Penelope. "Oh, I **do** hope that wasn't Miss Lilly's dinner!"

"Oh, dear," said Priscilla, laughing as she saw Angelina searching for some undamaged tomatoes, "I think it was!"

The Pinkpaws twins walked off with their noses in the air, and Angelina stamped her paws.

"Don't you worry about Miss Lilly," she called after them. "She'll have the best meal ever at my house! The best meal EVER!"

··· ~ ···

Later, Angelina was busy replacing the wild flowers with roses, and Mr Mouseling was practising playing Dacovian polkas on his fiddle.

Mrs Mouseling was making Corn Royale. "Angelina, where are the tomatoes?" she asked.

"Sorry, Mum, but I ... er ... dropped them," said Angelina, putting some books about Dacovia on the sideboard.

"Oh, well," said Mrs Mouseling. "I'll just have to use a tin of tomatoes, I suppose ..."

Just then, there was a knock at the door.

"She's here!" said Angelina.

··· ～ ···

The dinner didn't go very well. Everyone felt awkward.

Angelina tried to make conversation. "Er, did you leave Dacovia before Queen Tatiana came to power?" she asked.

"Oh, darlink, that was a long time before I was born!" said Miss Lilly. "Now, Mrs Mouseling, may I have another slice of your delicious malt bread?"

As Mrs Mouseling leant across the table with the bread, PING! a button flew off her dress,

and landed in Miss Lilly's soup bowl. PLOP!

"I'm sorry," said Mrs Mouseling. "Er, Angelina, could you get the Corn Royale?"

The Corn Royale was in such a tall casserole dish that Angelina couldn't see over the top of it. She tried to put it down on the sideboard, but put it on the pile of library books instead!

They wobbled, and the casserole dish crashed to the floor. SPLOSH! There was Corn Royale everywhere!

"Oh no!" said Angelina, and she burst into tears and rushed up to her bedroom.

That's where Miss Lilly found her a few minutes later. "Darlink, please don't cry," she said.

"But I wanted ... sob! ... everything to be wonderful," said Angelina. "But you didn't like the soup ... sob! ... and the Corn Royale is ruined ... sob! ... and ..."

"Darlink," said Miss Lilly, "I am **so** bored with Corn Royale."

"But I've ruined everything," said Angelina.

Miss Lilly shook her head. "You have ruined nothink! I am here with you and your family in your lovely cottage. What could be nicer?"

"The Mouseski Restaurant?"

said Angelina sadly.

"Pooh! Darlink, it's all politics there! Dacs and Ovians, so con-fu-sing!"

"But aren't you hungry?" asked Angelina.

"STARVINK!" said Miss Lilly.

Angelina grinned. "Do you like cheese pie?" she asked.

Miss Lilly nodded. "I just LOVE it!"

··· ~ ···

Later, after a delicious dinner of cheese pie, Mr Mouseling was playing Dacovian music when Miss Lilly interrupted him. "Please, no more of that! Play some jolly music that we can DANCE to!"

So he did ...

And they did!

Angelina's year: summer

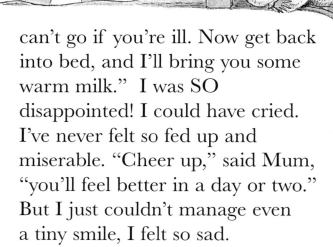

I just couldn't wait for the summer holidays to begin this year, because Mum said we could go to the seaside on the very first day after school finished. But guess what? When I woke up, I felt really ill. I was hot, and I was snuffling and sneezing and coughing. When I got out of bed my legs felt all wobbly, so I had to sit down on the edge of the bed and hold onto my doll.

Mum put her paw on my forehead. "You've got a bad cold," she said. "I'm sorry, Angelina. I know how much you were looking forward to our trip to the seaside, but we can't go if you're ill. Now get back into bed, and I'll bring you some warm milk." I was SO disappointed! I could have cried. I've never felt so fed up and miserable. "Cheer up," said Mum, "you'll feel better in a day or two." But I just couldn't manage even a tiny smile, I felt so sad.

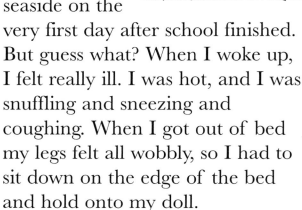

I was SO disappointed!

I stayed in bed all morning, but it felt like a whole year! Mum kept coming up to see how I was. She could see how sad I was about not being able to go to the seaside, so she came up with one of her brilliant ideas. "If you can't go to the seaside, we'll bring the seaside to you," she said. I couldn't imagine how she was going to do that, but Mum could. She was gone for a while, then she asked me to come downstairs.

What a great idea! I felt better already!

What a surprise! Mum had brought a deckchair in from the garden and filled it with lots of soft, squishy pillows. Then she sat me in it, and covered me up with a warm, comfy blanket. And that's not all – she brought my favourite toy, and filled a big basket with all my things, like my crayons and ballet books. "Now we can pretend we're at the seaside," said Mum, "and we'll go just as soon as you're feeling well again!" What a great idea! I felt better already!

Arthur the butterfly

1 It was a lovely summer's day, and much too hot for dancing class, so Miss Lilly took Angelina and her friends for a picnic in the woods.

2 William was wearing a paper napkin crown. "I'm Arthur!" he said. "King of earth and sky!" When a breeze blew the crown off, Angelina chased after it.

3 Angelina didn't find the napkin, but she did find a pink butterfly. "Oh, you're the most beautiful thing I've ever seen," she said, as the others arrived.

4 "He's beautiful! But why is he shaking?" said Alice. "It's his leg," said Angelina. "Look, I think it's broken. I'll take him home and look after him."

5 Angelina named the butterfly Arthur, and put him in a sweet jar. She filled it with flowers and leaves. Henry wanted to help, but Angelina wouldn't let him.

6 Angelina made special things for Arthur. There was a seat, and a swing. "I wonder what he'll need next?" said Angelina.

7 Alice knew. "He needs lots of sunshine and plenty of exercise," she read from a book about butterflies. "He should go home soon. His leg's better now."

8 "But he's still very ill, Alice!" said Angelina crossly. "He can't even fly yet!" Just then, Henry let out a yelp. "Yes he can!" he said. "Look! Arthur's flying!"

9 Arthur **was** flying. "I think you should let him go now," said Alice. "No, Alice!" said Angelina. "What if he hurts himself again? He'll be safer here with me."

10 As Henry peered into the jar, Arthur stopped flying, and sat on a leaf. "He does look sad," said Henry. "Maybe he doesn't like living in the sweet jar."

11 When Angelina and Alice went for lunch, Henry took the top off Arthur's jar, and out he fluttered. "Oops!" said Henry. "Come here, Arthur!"

12 But Arthur flew out of the window! When she found out, Angelina looked everywhere for him. Henry wanted to help, but Angelina told him to go away.

13 "I'll never see Arthur again," said Angelina, sobbing. "Never!" But when Henry said, "Maybe he's gone home to the woods?" Angelina rushed off: "YES!"

14 In the woods, Angelina saw something pink, and reached out to it. But she fell into a deep hole! "Hellpp!" said Angelina. "Get me out, Henry!"

15 Henry saw Angelina's paw, and grabbed it. But he fell into the hole, too – and landed on Angelina's head. "DON'T SAY A WORD," said Angelina.

16 "We're trapped!" said Henry, starting to cry. "What if they never find us?" Angelina felt sorry for him, and pulled him close. "It's OK, Henry," she said. "It's OK."

17 That night, Mr Mouseling led a search party for Angelina and Henry. When Alice spotted Arthur she said, "He's trying to tell us something! Follow him!"

18 As Arthur led them through the trees, Alice heard a cry, and ran towards it. But when she got to the hole, she fell in, too, and landed on Angelina and Henry!

19 "You're here to rescue us," said Angelina, "not to squash us!" That made Alice giggle. It made Henry giggle, too, and it wasn't long before Angelina joined in.

20 Mr Mouseling heard the giggles, and shone his torch into the hole. He laughed, too, when he saw the mouselings. "What have we here?" he said.

21 Just then, Miss Lilly arrived. Her coat was very dirty, and her boots were covered in mud. "Don't worry, my darlinks, I am here!" she said.

22 Next day, Angelina was in the garden, staring up at the sky, when Arthur landed on her nose! "You came back!" she cried, and Henry held out the jar.

23 Arthur flew onto Angelina's paw, but she didn't put him into the jar. She waved her paw, and off he fluttered. "Why did you do that?" asked Henry.

24 "Being trapped is awful – we know that," said Angelina. "I want Arthur to be happy, and to be happy he needs to be free. Bye, Arthur! Off you go!"

Summer fun

summer's fun because it's holiday time! Before we break up we always put on a big end-of-term show at ballet school.

Which of the things in the little pictures can you see in the big picture? Write a tick for 'yes' or a cross for 'no' in each circle.

The legend of Big Paw

1 It was autumn, and the Mouselings were camping in the Black Cat Hills. They were sitting around a camp fire, toasting marshmallows on sticks.

2 "Do you remember camping here when you were young?" Grandpa asked Maurice and Louis. "You lost my medal here, my Furforth Medal for Bravery."

3 Grandpa used a stick to draw a cross-shaped medal in the soil. "It was named after old Colonel Furforth. No one knows where he is now …"

4 "We were playing soldiers," Uncle Louis explained. "And you got us lost!" said Angelina's dad. "Yes, but Big Paw was chasing us!" said Uncle Louis.

5 "Who's Big Paw?" asked Angelina. "He's a giant black cat with green staring eyes," said Maurice. "And sharp fangs," added Uncle Louis.

6 Henry was worried. "Does he eat mouselings?" he asked. "No, Henry," said Grandpa. "There's no such thing as Big Paw. These two made him up!"

7 Next morning, when the sun was coming up and the others were still asleep, Angelina set off into the hills. She didn't see Henry tiptoeing after her ...

8 Angelina was walking up a narrow path when she heard a noise behind her. Henry had tripped and fallen. "What are you doing here?" asked Angelina.

9 "I've come to find Big Paw!" said Henry. "Well you'll have to go back," said Angelina. "I can't take you with me. I'm going to find Grandpa's medal."

10 But it was a long way back, and Angelina didn't want Henry to get lost. "All right, you can come," she said, and Henry ran to catch up with her.

11 Poor Henry! He tripped on another rock, and his camera rolled off the track and down the side of the mountain. "Oh, HENRY!" said Angelina.

12 Angelina and Henry climbed down the rocks to get his camera. But Henry slipped, bumped into Angelina, and they **both** slid down a muddy slope!

13 Down they fell, bump-bump-bump, all the way to the bottom of the hill. Henry found his camera – but Angelina couldn't find the way back up!

14 Angelina walked down one of the paths. "Which way now?" asked Henry. Angelina looked at her map, which was covered in mud. "This way!"

15 Suddenly, Angelina stumbled into a hole in the track. "Look, a paw print, and it's as big as a mouse!" said Henry. "Rubbish!" said Angelina. "Come on!"

16 Much later, on another path, Henry pointed to another giant paw print. Then they heard a loud noise: **MEEOOW**! "Run!" cried Angelina.

17 Angelina and Henry ran until they came to a clearing. **MEEOOW**! Angelina saw a tiny cave entrance. "Quick!" she said. "We'll hide in there!"

18 **MEEOOW**! "It's all right," said Angelina. "Big Paw is much too big to get in here." But just then, they saw a shadow outside the cave. **MEEOOW**!

19 Angelina and Henry backed away from the shadow – and fell over a ledge! They were in a deep, dark hollow, and the shadow was above them ...

20 A paw reached out of the dark towards them – but it wasn't a big paw, it was just a normal mouse-sized paw. "Colonel Furforth at your service," said a voice.

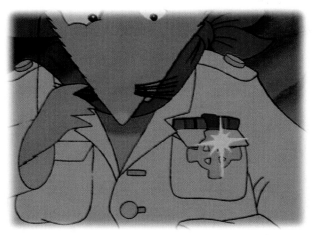

21 Angelina looked up, and saw an old mouse wearing a medal like the one Grandpa had drawn. "What are you doing with Grandpa's medal?" she asked.

22 Angelina found out later, back at the campsite. "So YOU were Big Paw," said Uncle Louis. "Yes," said the colonel. "I made the **MEOWS** with my megaphone."

23 When they got back home, Angelina, Henry and Grandpa looked at some of Henry's pictures. "What's that big shadow behind Colonel Furforth?" asked Grandpa.

24 "It's a cat!" said Henry. "See? It's Big Paw!" Angelina shook her head. "No it isn't, Henry," she said. Henry nodded his head. "It is!" he said. "**IS**! **IS**! **IS**!"

Angelina's year: autumn

Miss Lilly always likes to put on a big autumn show at the ballet school. This year it was called Falling Leaves – and we were the leaves! Miss Lilly taught us how to flutter and twirl across the practice room.

It was hard work – but lots of fun! She didn't let us stop until we had all the steps just right! "Once again, please, darlinks!" she called. "Practice makes perfect!"

Dad said we all looked so lovely, and danced so well, that he put us on the front page of the Mouseland Gazette!

Henry had a part in the show, too. Isn't his leaf outfit sweet?

It was my cousin Henry's birthday in October. I'd been saving up my pocket money for weeks, and on the day before his party, Alice and I jumped on our bikes and cycled to Mrs Thimble's shop to buy him a present. He got lots and lots of nice things, but he said the toy train I gave him was the very best!

Wheeee! Over we go!

Alice and I both love doing cartwheels!

Autumn fun

I like autumn because it's the season when there are all kinds of yellow, gold and brown leaves to play with!

1

50

These two autumn pictures look the same, but there are five things that are different in picture 2. Can you spot them all?

51

Angelina and Anya

It was autumn in Chipping Cheddar, and Angelina and Alice were looking for blackberries.

"How many have you found?" asked Angelina.

"None!" said Alice.

"Me neither," said Angelina, looking at the blackberry bushes. "I don't understand it. Last autumn these bushes were full of blackberries."

"I know," said Alice. "I ate three baskets of them all in one go!"

"Let's try again," said Angelina, going deeper into the bushes.

Angelina didn't find any blackberries, but she did find a little harvest mouse, who stared at Angelina for a second, then turned and ran away.

··· ~ ···

At school, all the mouselings were talking about blackberries.

"Someone must have picked them all," said Sammy.

"But who would do that?" said William.

Penelope and Priscilla, the Pinkpaws twins, looked at each other.

"But they don't belong to anyone, do they?" said Priscilla.

"That's the whole point," said Angelina. "They belong to **everyone**."

"It ... er ... must have been those harvest mice camping in the field," said Penelope.

"Yes," said Priscilla. "Mother says they can't be trusted."

Just then Miss Chalk arrived with a new pupil. "This is Anya Moussorsky," she said. "She'll be here for a few weeks while her parents help with the harvest. Angelina will look after you, Anya."

"It's the mouse we saw near the blackberry bushes!" Angelina whispered to Alice.

As Anya sat down next to Angelina, Sammy took out his peashooter, and a pea hit the back of Anya's head. He laughed.

"Odd Ears!" Priscilla added.

··· ~ ···

In the break, Angelina watched Anya on the rope swing. She was very good.

"It's like flying!" said Anya.

"I haven't been on a swing since we left Dacovia."

"Dacovia?" said Angelina. "My ballet teacher, Miss Lilly, is from Dacovia!"

"I dance too," said Anya. "Not ballet though."

Just then, along came Priscilla, Penelope and Sammy.

"You shouldn't hang around with thieves, Angelina," said Priscilla.

"What are you talking about?" Angelina replied.

Penelope pointed at Anya. "Her family stole all the blackberries!"

"No!" said Anya. "It was not us. A lady with a red scarf took them."

"Just like a harvest mouse to fib," said Penelope.

"Yes," added Priscilla. "Why don't you go back to where you came from?"

"Yeah, go on, Odd Ears!" said Sammy.

··· ~ ···

After school, Anya was waiting for her mother to pick her up.

"Shall we wait with her?" Angelina asked Alice.

"If we do that we'll be late for ballet," said Alice. "And you know how Miss Lilly feels about that."

"Come on then," said Angelina.

That night, Angelina was helping her mum make some cakes for the school fair. She told her about Anya. "She's nice ... but some of the others were mean to her."

"Then she's lucky to have a friend like you to stick up for her, Angelina," said Mrs Mouseling.

Angelina felt ashamed. She **hadn't** stuck up for Anya!

The next day, Anya wasn't in school, and Angelina decided to find out why, so she went to the Moussorsky family's camp.

Anya was in her tent, in bed.

"Are you ill?" asked Angelina

"No, but I didn't want to go to school today, so I said I wasn't feeling well," Anya replied.

Angelina took a deep breath. "I'm sorry about yesterday. I should have said something. I should have been a better friend."

"It's all right," said Anya. "It always happens. It's because I have to move from school to school."

Angelina looked around and pointed to Anya's special dancing costume. "Will you show me?" she asked.

Anya put on her costume and danced for Angelina. She played a tambourine and Mr Moussorsky played an accordion.

"That was wonderful!" said Angelina. "Will you teach me?"

Anya nodded. "Of course I will!"

Later, Mrs Moussorsky brought scones and jam for Angelina and Anya. "I'm sorry it's not blackberry jam," she said. "We couldn't find a single berry, could we, Anya?"

"No," said Anya. "That lady must have picked them all."

"This lady," said Angelina, "will you show me where she was?"

Anya and Angelina went to the blackberry bushes. "She was around here," said Anya. "She

wore a red scarf with blue flowers, like ..."

"Like this one?" said Angelina, taking a scarf that was hooked on a blackberry bush, and Anya nodded.

··· ~ ···

Next day, at school, Angelina showed Alice, William and Sammy the scarf. "If we find out who owns the scarf, we find the person who took all the blackberries," said Angelina.

Along came the Pinkpaws twins. "What are you doing with our mother's scarf?" Penelope said to Anya.

"You thief!" said Priscilla.

"It's not Anya who's the thief!" said Angelina.

"It was your mother who

picked the blackberries," said Anya.

"Well, what if she did?" said Penelope. "You said they belonged to everyone."

"Anyway, she's making blackberry jelly for the school fair," said Priscilla.

··· ~ ···

But on the day of the fair, no one bought Mrs Pinkpaws' blackberry jelly.

"It's burnt," said Mrs Hodgepodge. "If you're going to take all the blackberries, you might at least make some decent jelly!"

There was a special concert in the school gym. Angelina and Anya danced together as Mr Moussorsky played his accordion and Mr Mouseling played his fiddle. It was a great success, and Angelina and

Anya became good friends.

··· ~ ···

A few weeks later, it was time for Anya and her family to leave Chipping Cheddar.

"I wish you weren't leaving, Anya," said Angelina.

"So do I," said Anya. "But I'll be back next autumn."

"Promise?" said Angelina.

"**Promise**!" said Anya.

Angelina's year: winter

Some people just don't like winter. Not me! I love the cold, crisp days – and this year I had a lovely new hat and scarf set to wear.

Grandma knitted it for me, and she chose just the right colour of red to match my ice-skates. Perfect!

As soon as Miller's Pond froze over, I called for Alice, and we went skating. I wasn't the only mouseling with new clothes this year – Alice had some, too, a lovely green coat with a hood trimmed with white fur, to match her new skates. Do you like her scarf?

Cousin Henry wanted to come skating with us, of course. The only problem is that he's not very good at it. "Skating is just like dancing, Henry," I told him. "The only difference is that it's on a very slippery surface." Poor Henry! He spent more time sitting on his bottom than he did gliding around on the ice!

Wonderful, my darlinks! You look marvellous!

I love Christmas! We always put on an extra-special show at Miss Lilly's ballet school. We rehearsed for weeks, so that on Christmas Eve everyone was ready. This year the show was called "Christmas Fairies", and it was **so** much fun to dance! We wore special dresses (mine was a pale peach colour) that had matching flowers round the neck and the hem. When we all danced across the stage on points, waving sprays of flowers, Miss Lilly was **so** pleased with us.

"Wonderful, my darlinks!" she said. "You look marvellous!" She looked pretty marvellous herself – but then she always does!

Miss Lilly had a prize for the best Flower Fairy, and guess what – it was me! I couldn't wait to get my ballerina doll home!

Isn't she the cutest thing?

No match for Angelina

1 It was winter, and Chipping Cheddar was lying under a thick white blanket of snow. The mouselings were having lots of fun on the frozen pond.

2 The mouselings were enjoying a game of Icepuck. They skated as fast as they could across the ice, trying to hit the puck into the goal.

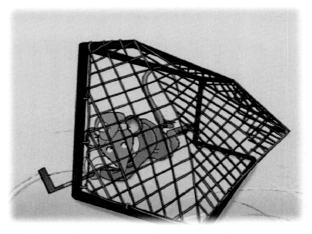

3 "I've got it!" said one. "No, I have!" said another. But just then, Angelina skated up with her Icepuck stick. "Don't count on it!" she yelled.

4 Angelina raced across the ice, guiding the puck with her stick. Then she hit the puck as hard as she could – and it flew into the net. GOAL!

5 The other players cheered, and patted her on the back. But Sammy wasn't pleased. He threw down his stick and glared at her. "Show-off!"

6 After the game, Sammy's dad had some news for the skaters. "We've been asked to take part in the Mouseland Icepuck Tournament."

7 "WOW!" The mouselings were very excited. "I'm going to choose the team tomorrow morning," said Sammy's dad, "so be here early."

8 Next morning, Angelina was back at the pond. But Sammy wasn't pleased to see her. "Why are **you** here?" he asked. "We can't have a **girl** on the team!"

9 When she got home, Angelina burst into tears. "They won't let me play!" she sobbed. "No girls allowed. What a stupid rule! It's just not fair!"

10 Angelina was putting her stick into the cupboard when she saw her dad's old Icepuck helmet and jersey. "I'm just borrowing these, Dad," she said, all smiles again.

11 Angelina put on her dad's kit and went back to the pond. The boys were still there. "We need one more player for the team," said Sammy's dad.

12 Angelina skated across the pond at speed, turned, and came to a perfect stop. "You're on the team, er ..." said Sammy's dad. "I'm ... er ... Andy," said Angelina!

13 From that day, sometimes Angelina was Angelina, and sometimes she was Andy. In the Icepuck kit, no one guessed that Andy was really Angelina.

14 On the day of the big game, Angelina sat with her parents. "Er, I'm just going for a drink," she said, and she rushed off to put on her Icepuck kit.

15 Angelina's helmet strap broke, but there was no time to fix it. She skated out onto the ice just before the whistle blew for the start of the game.

16 It was a great game, and Angelina scored more points than any other player. At half-time the score was Chipping Cheddar 10, Little Brie 3.

17 In the changing room, Angelina bent to pick up a puck – and her helmet fell off! "Angelina?" said Sammy. "You can't play in this game!"

18 Angelina had to sit on the bench to watch the second half. When the scores were level, Chipping Cheddar got a penalty. But who was going to take it?

19 Sammy knew Angelina was the best player, and he skated over to her. "Go on," he said, and she skated onto the ice. "ANDY! ANDY!" chanted the crowd.

20 Angelina prepared to take the shot, then she stopped, and took off her helmet. The crowd gasped. "Look! It's Angelina!" said Mr Mouseling.

21 Angelina hit the puck and it flew into the net. GOAL! Angelina's team lifted her into the air. "Chipping Cheddar win 11-10!" said the commentator.

22 Next day, Angelina's picture was on the front page of the Mouseland Gazette. "Ballerina makes history," read Alice. "You're famous!"

23 "Well, that 'no girls allowed' rule was silly," said Angelina. "Someone had to change it, didn't they? I was just lucky that it was me."

24 That made Angelina think. "You know, I might run for President of Mouseland one day ..." she said. Alice giggled. "Oh, **Angelina**!"

Winter fun

Winter is the season of dark nights, white snow, warm fires – and lots of presents at Christmas time!

This year, one of Angelina's presents is a jigsaw puzzle made from a favourite photograph. Which three jigsaw pieces will complete it?

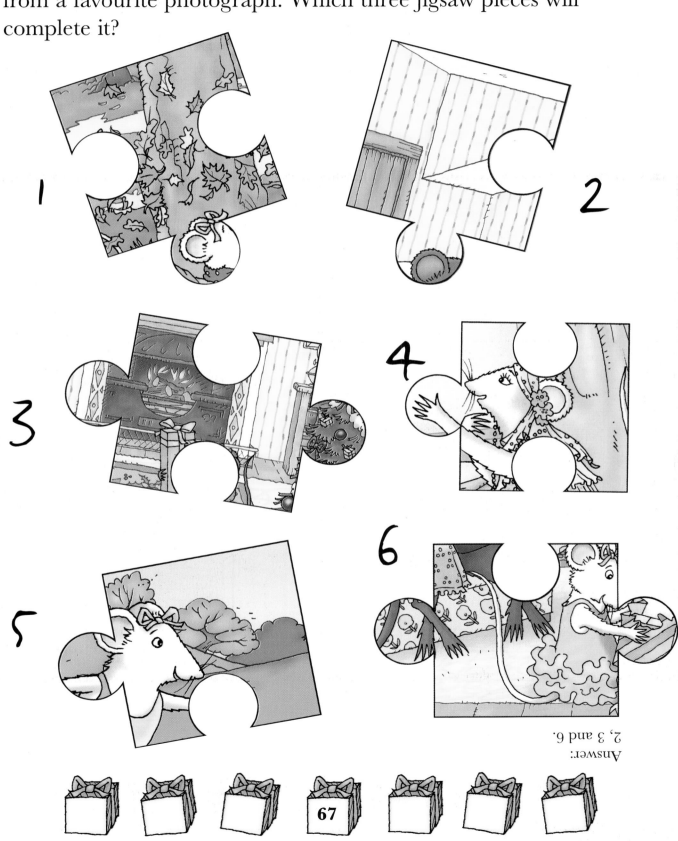

Answer: 2, 3 and 6.

All about Angelina

Can you answer all twelve questions about Angelina and her friends? The answers are at the bottom of page 69.

1 In the story 'No match for Angelina' on page 60, what game did Angelina play?

2 What colour is Angelina's front door? Is it:
a blue
b yellow or
c red?

3 Mrs Hodgepodge owns the village shop. True or false?

4 In the story called 'The ballerina rag doll' on page 16, what was the name of the doll?

5 What is Angelina's sister called? Is her name:
a Holly
b Polly or
c Molly?

6 What was the name of Angelina's pink butterfly?

7 In the story called 'The legend of Big Paw' on page 42, who won a Furforth Medal for Bravery?

8 What is the name of the village where Angelina lives?

9 The Pinkpaws twins are called Pamela and Patsy. True or false?

10 What is Alice's last name? Is it:
a Twinkletoes
b Shinyshoes or
c Nimbletoes?

11 What is the name of Angelina's cousin?

12 Which country does Miss Lilly come from?

Answers:
1. Icepuck; 2. c red; 3. False; Mrs Thimble owns the shop; 4. Polka; 5. b Polly; 6. Arthur; 7. Grandpa; 8. Chipping Cheddar; 9. False, their names are Penelope and Priscilla; 10. c Nimbletoes; 11. Henry; 12. Da...

69